PACIFIC COAST

Volume 2

Tales of the Wild West Series

Rick Steber

Illustrations by Don Gray

NOTE
Pacific Coast is the second book in the
Tales of the Wild West Series.

Pacific Coast
Volume 2
Tales of the Wild West Series

Bonanza Publishing
Box 204
Prineville, Oregon 97754

INTRODUCTION

Sir Francis Drake, the daring English pirate, was the first European to sail the stormy North Pacific. In 1579, after having raided the Spanish settlements of South America, he sought to escape up the coast through an inland waterway that would return his ship, the *Golden Hind*, to the Atlantic Ocean.

In his wake came other explorers. They soon concluded a Northwest Passage did not exist and turned attention to exploiting the natural resources of the region. Trade was initiated with the natives, trinkets for sea otter fur. The fur was transported to China where riches beyond the wildest dreams awaited the adventuresome sailors.

Within a decade the sea otter played out and mountain men pushed inland, trading and trapping beaver. The great fur companies, Hudson's Bay, North West and Pacific Fur fought for the rich spoils.

The discovery of gold in California signaled the start of a new era. Miners flooded to the Sierra Nevada mountains. Eventually they became disillusioned with the diggings and drifted north, discovering veins of gold in rock and placer pockets in creek bottoms and even on ocean beaches.

Following the miners came a wave of pioneers who settled the interior valleys, laid claim to the land and plowed the virgin soil. A few hardy souls pushed over the last mountain range, going as far west as land allowed. They were rugged individualists who ever after were isolated by the deep woods on one side and the wide Pacific on the other.

SIR FRANCIS DRAKE

Sir Francis Drake, after having plundered the riches of South America, sought to escape in the Pacific rather than run the gauntlet across the Atlantic ocean. He pointed his ship, the *Golden Hind*, north in hope of discovering a Northwest Passage that would lead him back to England.

The *Golden Hind* was the first European ship to sail along the North Pacific coast, a land Drake called *Nova Albion* (New England). By summer the pirate ship was reported to be in the vicinity of 48 degrees north latitude (near Vancouver Island). Here a massive cold front moved in and froze the rigging. The crew, fresh from the Tropics, implored their captain to turn back.

Drake reluctantly ordered his ship south. It is known the *Golden Hind,* under the weight of tons of plunder and leaking at the seams, put in at a harbor along the coast for repairs; a brass plaque found near San Francisco Bay in 1936 is considered by many to prove this was the site of the layover while other historians believe the actual harbor was Whale's Cove on the Oregon coast.

After spending more than a month making repairs, the *Golden Hind* put to sea. Drake pointed his ship into the trade winds and, fourteen months after departing the coast of Nova Albion, the *Golden Hind* sailed into Plymouth Sound, England, her keel having completed a furrow that circled the globe.

DISCOVERING THE COLUMBIA

At 4 a.m. on May 11, 1792, Captain Robert Gray and his ship, the *Columbia Rediviva*, stood off the entrance of a great river. The ship's log noted the wind was blowing strong out of the west, breakers were visible running in a line from shore to shore, and there appeared no visible opening.

Gray carefully scanned the bar, located the safest point to cross and ordered sails set. According to the ship's log, "At 8 a.m., being a little windward of the entrance to the harbor, bore away, and run in east-northeast, between breakers, having from five to seven fathoms of water. When we were over the bar we found this to be a large river of fresh water, up which we steered. Many canoes came alongside. At 1 p.m. came to with the small bower, in two fathoms, black and white sand. The entrance between the bars bore west-southwest, distant ten miles. The north side of the river a half-mile distant from the ship; the south side the same, two and a half miles distance .... natives came alongside. People employed in pumping the salt water out of our water casks, in order to fill with fresh, while the ship floated in. So ends."

The "Great River of the West" had been discovered. And Captain Gray claimed it for the United States of America and named it after his ship, the Columbia.

3

FIRST WHITE MEN

Long, long ago a Clatsop woman was walking along the beach near the mouth of the Columbia River. She came upon a shocking sight; a sailing ship had run aground during the night and the surf was battering it. Two white men came toward her. She was very frightened, ran away to her village where she told her people that she had seen men with white skin.

The tribe cautiously approached the survivors and at first believed them to be spirits who lived on the far side of the ocean where the sun slept. The white men made sign they were friendly and even heated corn over a fire and gave the Indians their first taste of popcorn.

The two were taken to the Clatsop village and given the names of Kunupi and Soto. In return for the tribe's hospitality they taught the Indians to forge metal from the shipwreck into useful tools.

According to the Indian legend, Kunupi and Soto spoke about returning to their homeland and one day they headed upriver and were never seen again. When Lewis and Clark arrived at the mouth of the Columbia River in 1805 they found the Clatsop tribe to be a very powerful nation, advanced in the use of forging metal for ornaments, tools and weapons. They claimed this knowledge came from shipwrecked white men.

At the turn of this century a stone head was unearthed on the lower Columbia River. It had been sculpted in the likeness of a Caucasian man. The stone, eaten and discolored by lichen, was put on display at Maryhill Museum. Could it be the face of Kunupi or Soto?

SHANGHAIED

Portland was infamous as the leading West Coast port in the trafficking of shanghaied sailors. And the most ruthless of all shanghaiers was Bunco Kelly.

One time Bunco stole the wooden Indian from in front of Wildman's Tobacco Shop and smuggled him aboard a British bark. He charged the customary fifty dollars and admonished the captain, "Don't disturb him. He's sleeping. He'll sober up by the time you hit Astoria."

Bunco really earned his reputation the night he happened on thirty sailors who had been drinking at the Snug Harbor Saloon on Second and Morrison. After it closed, they had broken into the building next door where they tapped a keg of what they presumed to be strong spirits. They drank freely. It was their final drink; the basement was rented to Johnson & Son Undertakers and embalming fluid was stored in the keg. Bunco gathered the bodies, loaded them in the back of a couple hacks and carted them off to a waiting ship where he collected his finders fee, telling the ship's captain his new sailors were "dead drunk".

At the height of Portland's shanghaiing days the crimps charged as much as $135 per man and boasted they had the harbor master, chief of police and mayor in their hind pockets. But the sailing era began to fade as the steamship became more popular. Large crews were no longer needed. And then came World War I and all the able-bodied men went off to war. By the 1920s the Portland waterfront was a relatively safe place; a man no longer needed to worry about waking up with a hangover and finding himself a hundred miles out to sea.

HUNTING THE WHALE

Whales migrate south in the fall and north in spring. In the distant past Makah Indians hunted the whales as they migrated along the Pacific coast.

The hunt began with strong paddlers maneuvering a large, cedar canoe near a whale. When the bow was within a few feet the harpooner would thrust his harpoon deep. The paddlers pulled hard to avoid the dangerous, thrashing tail as the whale dove and headed to the open sea. The canoe, sometimes shooting ahead at great speed, was linked to the whale by a long, woven kelp rope.

Each time the whale came to the surface to spout, the harpooner would drive in a lance. Attached to the bone-tipped lance was a seal-skin bladder filled with air. And as more lances found their marks it became increasingly difficult for the whale to dive.

It was a simple and cruel method the Indians used for hunting the whale. The struggle might last for days. The ocean would run red with blood, the whale would shriek, moan and cry. Its mate would circle, calling, calling. Eventually, unless weather and high seas forced the Indians ashore, the whale would die.

Now the most exhausting work began as the paddlers slowly towed the bulky weight toward shore. The final action of tide and surf would help deposit the carcass on the beach. Then the Indian women labored to cut the blubber into strips to be used for cooking, smoking and rendering.

Successful hunters were held in high esteem by the tribe. In the late 1700s, when white men began visiting the coast, the best Indian whale hunter was said to have killed 59 whales in his lifetime.

FATE OF THE *TONQUIN*

To assure the success of the fledgling Pacific Fur Company, John Jacob Astor sent two expeditions to the West Coast; one by land and the other by sea. His ship, the *Tonquin,* departed from New York on September 8, 1810, rounded the Horn and arrived at the mouth of the Columbia River on March 11, 1811.

The *Tonquin* unloaded a detachment of men to begin building Fort Astoria and then continued north up the coast. The following story was told by a Chinook Indian, an eyewitness named Lamazee: "We remained (in a harbor on Vancouver Island) for some days, Indians going and coming, but not much trade. One day Indians came on board in great numbers, but did not trade much although they had plenty of skins. The prices offered did not please the Indians, so they carried back their furs....

"Next day the Indians came off to trade in great numbers. On their coming alongside, the Captain ordered the boarding netting to be put up around the ship, and would not allow more than ten on board at a time; but just as the trade had commenced, an Indian was detected cutting the boarding-netting with a knife. On being detected he instantly jumped into one of the canoes which were alongside and made his escape.... Next day, the offender was brought to the ship and delivered up.... Indians began to flock about the ship.... The conflict was bloody but short. The savages, with their naked knives and horrid yells, rushed the unsuspecting and defenseless whites, who were dispersed all over the ship, and in five minutes' time the vessel was their own.... (The ship) blew up in the air with a fearful explosion, filling the whole place with broken fragments and mutilated bodies. Stephen Weeks (the armorer) must have been the man who blew up the ship and all that remained, and by that awful act of revenge 175 Indians perished...."

STAR OF OREGON

During the early 1800s the Hudson's Bay Company owned just about everything there was to own in the Oregon Country: trading posts, transportation, livestock....

But Joseph Gale, a retired sailor and mountain man, set out to break the Company's monopoly. He conceived a plan to build a schooner in Oregon, sail it to California, sell it, purchase livestock and drive the animals to the Willamette Valley.

Gale selected Swan Island in the lower Willamette River as his building site and began work on a vessel in the fall of 1840. By the following spring the *Star of Oregon* was launched and the vessel spent the next year being outfitted for sea near Willamette Falls.

The schooner was 53 feet 8 inches in overall length and had a beam of 10 feet 9 inches. The frame was constructed of swamp white oak and she was planked with red cedar. She had a fore and main sail as well as a flying jib.

The voyage to the Pacific began August 27, 1842. Captain Gale chose to teach his green crew, which included two farmers, two mountain men and a boy, the rudiments of sailing as they traveled down river. It was not until the middle of September that the captain thought his ship and crew fit to challenge the dangerous, rocky coast.

They found the ocean to be stormy and rough. The crew became seasick. Captain Gale took over and during one 36-hour stretch he never left the helm.

The *Star of Oregon* was sailed into San Francisco harbor and Captain Gale sold her to a French captain. The following spring Gale started overland driving 1,250 head of cattle, 600 horses and mules and nearly 300 sheep. Two months later the caravan arrived in the Willamette Valley. The days of the Hudson's Bay Company's stranglehold on the Oregon Country was over.

KEEP THE LIGHT BURNING

"Wake up! It's midnight, time for your shift. Sure one heck of a gale blowin'."

George Easterbrook, third assistant keeper of the light at Cape Disappointment on the north shore of the Columbia River, shook the sleep from his head. He started toward the lighthouse, into the teeth of one of the worst storms he had ever seen. The wind howled and rain stung his face as he was forced to crawl on his hands and knees to keep from being blown into the sea. At last he reached the base of the stone tower, filled a can with oil to replenish the lantern and climbed the winding stairs.

He quickly went about his normal tasks -- filling the oil reservoir, winding the clockwork machinery which kept the pump working, polishing the heavy glass prisms and all the windows inside. At last one job remained -- wiping the salt spray from the outside of the windows. He bravely stepped onto the balcony, remembering to take an extra towel with him. The doorknob had been broken for the past several weeks and the door could not be opened from the outside. Just as he reached for the towel to stuff in the jamb, a gust of wind tore the door from his hand, slammed it shut.

There he was, stranded 80 feet from the ground with no possibility of help until sunrise. Worse yet, in two hours the clocks would wind down and the light would go out. George went ahead and polished the windows, hoping one of the other men would come check on him, knowing they were all sleeping at this time of the night. More than an hour passed and then the wind slackened. He seized the opportunity to don his buckskin gloves, grabbed hold of the copper wire that acted as a lightning rod and stepped over the railing.

Halfway to the ground a gust swung him out over the raging sea and sent him crashing back against the tower. He managed to hold on and was finally able to drop to the ground. He crawled back to the door, climbed the steps, rewound the clocks and then fainted.

SS BEAVER

It has been nearly a century since she went to Davy Jones's locker but as long as ships float and sailors man them there will be talk of the *SS Beaver*.

The *Beaver* was built for use in the Pacific Northwest by the Hudson's Bay Company in Blackwall, London, England, and was launched on the Thames River in 1835 before King William IV, his royal court and an estimated 150,000 Englishmen.

She was a unique ship with engines and boilers built by one of the inventors of the steam engine, James Watt. The hull was constructed of English oak and African teak and all the joints were fitted together "with copper bolts and oak treenails".

The two 13-foot paddle wheels were stowed in the hold and the *Beaver* was sailed as a brig to the Pacific. According to the ship's log, "We stood in for the Columbia Bar" on March 19, 1836 after a voyage of 163 days.

The *Beaver* was outfitted to operate on steam and on the last day of May she made a run as far upriver as the mouth of the Willamette. Less than a month later, with crewmen feeding chunks of Douglas fir into the firebox and the twin paddle wheels turning at 30 revolutions per minute, the *Beaver* crossed the Columbia Bar and became the first ship to steam into the Pacific.

The *Beaver* was used in the fur trade, ducking into inlets where the crew traded with the natives. Later she was used to transport miners to the big gold strike in British Columbia.

In 1888, after 52 years of faithful service, the *Beaver* steamed from Vancouver harbor into the Strait of Georgia. She was under very light steam when she was caught in a treacherous current and pushed onto a rocky point. There she lay, on the rocks at the entrance of the harbor, until May 26, 1892 when the stern-wheeler *Yosemite*, the pride of the modern ocean liners, passed near. Her wake caused a swell that washed the *Beaver* off the rocks and to her final grave.

NOT GUILTY

Edward Gardner was a hermit. He hunted and fished in the Coast range and came to town only when he ran low on tobacco. It was tobacco that nearly cost him his freedom.

Gardner smoked a pipe. One time he tapped the ashes out on a rock and went on about his business. At a later date he discovered a fire had burned three acres of underbrush around the rock.

Someone else was in the woods that day, saw Gardner tap out the ashes and turned him in to authorities for causing a forest fire. Gardner was named in a secret grand jury indictment in Portland. Eventually news reached the southern Oregon coast and Gardner decided to come in on his own. He hiked to Grants Pass, the nearest railhead, and took the train north. In Portland he went before Judge Bean in U.S. District Court.

"I heard you was lookin' for me," he told the judge.

Judge Bean searched the file. "Gardner, Edward G. Yes, here it is. The charge is willfully setting fire to a large section of the Siskiyou National Forest. And how do you wish to plead?"

Gardner pulled himself straight. "Not guilty, your Honor." He explained the fire had destroyed only underbrush and had burned itself out in three acres. He told how he had walked 127 miles to the railhead and taken the train another 200 miles to turn himself in. He concluded by stating, "I didn't start the fire on purpose. It was an accident."

The judge drew a long breath and said, "Be more careful in the future, Mr. Gardner. Case dismissed."

UNDER THE BED

Ren Smith and his family lived near the ocean in the southwest corner of Oregon. It was tradition every fall that the men would take an extended hunting trip into the coast range and stock up on a winter's supply of meat.

One year Ren and his two sons, Tom and George, set off for an abandoned cabin in the area where they planned to hunt. The cabin had a good roof, bunks and a sheet metal stove. It would make a comfortable base camp.

The Smiths hiked all day and reached the cabin just as it was getting dark. The boys rustled up wood and Ren started a fire. George and Tom rested on a couple of the bunks while their father cooked dinner. The door to the stove was open and the fire cast a yellow glow inside the cabin.

Perhaps Tom subconsciously heard the sounds of rapid breathing coming from under his bunk, or maybe it was only his inquisitive nature that made him lean over, lift the corner of the blanket and peer under the bed. Two eyes stared back at him, eyes burning like embers.

He lost his grip on the blanket and in one tremendous leap propelled himself off the bed and to the far side of the room. "There's, there's something under there!" he sputtered.

Ren checked, found a cougar and dispatched it with a single shot from his rifle. When he pulled it from beneath the bunk he discovered the cat was very old, toothless and gaunt. Evidently it had crawled under the bunk to die. And it did.

14

SAVING THE CORN

Two men, Hansard Bessey and William Walker, were working in a sawmill along the Klamath River when they decided to strike out on their own. They hiked as far north as Roseburg but it was the middle of summer and very hot. To avoid the oppressive heat they headed for the coast. Along South Coos River they found reasonably priced farm ground and purchased adjoining acreage.

The following spring, 1887, they invested in a quantity of corn seed and planted a large crop. But before they had finished planting, thousands of free-loading blue jays arrived. They circled overhead and, when the farmers turned their backs, they swooped low and stole the corn seed. Scarecrows were put in the field but the birds ignored them. And when the corn began to sprout it made the pickings all the easier for the gluttonous jays.

"We're going to have to do something," Walker told his companion. Bessey volunteered to travel to Marshfield (Coos Bay) and purchase poison. He returned early the next morning and while he slept Walker mixed the strychnine with corn and set it on a broad stump.

The blue jaws swarmed around and by noon all the poisoned corn was gone, but it did not have any noticeable effect on the birds. Then Walker heard a great uproar coming from the vicinity of the river. He went to investigate and found the river littered with dead jays. Apparently after having gorged themselves on the poisoned corn the birds had gone for a drink of water. And now they were squawking loudly and dropping out of the trees. The corn crop was saved.

STATE OF JEFFERSON

The land between the Umpqua River on the north and the Trinity Alps to the south has at one time or another been under the control of Spain, England, Russia, Mexico and the United States. But residents of the territory now governed by bureaucrats in Sacramento and Salem have often dreamed of forming their own state.

The first serious effort to establish a new state began with a bill introduced into the 1852 California legislature. The residents were revolting against high taxes, poor mail service and the lack of adequate military protection. They felt they would be better off on their own.

One area newspaper pleaded the case, "This new state presents a country of uniform character and is distinct from the rest of either California or Oregon. Let our local resources be developed by a government identified with our locality; let us have a voice in the national councils where we can urge upon Congress our wants."

The bill died in legislative committee, just as other such attempts have failed in succeeding years. It seems that once every generation some would-be politician tries to rekindle the fire of revolution. Such was the case with the State of Jefferson.

The State of Jefferson gained national attention in November 1941 when residents of Yreka, California set road blocks on U.S. Highway 99 to interrogate travelers crossing the Jefferson "state line". But the Japanese invasion of Pearl Harbor cut short the life of the fledgling state. Today the spirit of the State of Jefferson lies dormant in the hearts of its citizens.

CLUBFOOT

Clubfoot was named after he left three toes in a steel trap the fall of 1858. From that date forward, the big grizzly was a marauding killer. He terrorized miners and settlers in the Klamath and Siskiyou mountains, killing their livestock and always leaving behind a plate-sized track with three toes missing.

A bounty was placed on Clubfoot's head and though he was chased many times the hunters were never able to catch him. One such incident began after Clubfoot had killed a number of sheep, not for food, but because of his lust for killing.

The best hunters and the finest hounds were gathered and followed a trail leading from the Siskiyous, across the upper end of the Rogue River valley, to Dead Indian country and beyond to the Cascades. Finally on the rim overlooking Crater Lake, after having covered more than 75 miles, the party gave up. They did not know it at the time, but as they turned toward home Clubfoot was following them. That night he killed a yearling steer within a mile of their camp.

Clubfoot continued his rampage until the spring of 1890. As he emerged from his winter's sleep two men, William Wright and Pearl Bean, killed him. The old bear had a standing measurement of nine feet and a reach exceeding twelve feet. Even after his hibernation he tipped the scales at 1,850 pounds. Clubfoot was exhibited locally and then shipped to the Columbian Exposition in Chicago. Later he toured Europe as part of a North American wildlife exhibit.

GRAVE MISTAKE

Back in the 1850s Indians along the Rogue River were threatened by an influx of miners, leftovers from the California 49ers who drifted north. Some of these men were outlaws and renegades. To them an Indian's life was expendable and if they happened upon a lone Indian they would often shoot him. After such an outrage the Indians would organize a war party to avenge the murder and yet another killing would take place. The vicious cycle went round and round.

In 1856 Indians attacked the settlement of Ellensburg (Gold Beach) and retreated upriver in canoes. A group of miners gave chase. They rode horseback and, trying to outflank the Indians, they returned to the Rogue River near the mouth of Lobster Creek. They took a commanding position on the rocky cliffs.

In time two canoes, loaded with Indians, came into view. The miners waited until the canoes were directly below the cliff before opening fire. There was no escape for the Indians. Later it was discovered the Indians they had killed that day at Lobster Creek were not even from the same tribe who had attacked the settlement.

LONE SURVIVOR

November 13, 1910, the ship *SS Czarina* was outbound from Marshfield (Coos Bay), her hold loaded with coal, cement and lumber destined for San Francisco. C.J. Dugan was in command of the ship and crew of 23.

Storm warnings had been posted along the coast, but Captain Dugan did not heed them. His ship was seaworthy and had breasted many fierce storms in her 27 years.

Rain rattled the windows. The *Czarina* poked her bow into the initial wave rolling over the Coos Bay bar and came up like a dog shaking water. Another wave hit and briny green water poured across the deck.

"Hard starboard," barked the captain. A swell caught the *Czarina*, sent her reeling toward the north jetty. Steering failed! "Drop anchor!" came the quick command. But the anchor did not hold. "Full ahead!"

A huge breaker lifted the heavy ship and tossed her as if she were an insignificant piece of driftwood. The *Czarina* went aground. Waves swept over her.

Word of the terrible disaster spread quickly and people came to watch the death of the *Czarina*. They witnessed survivors crawling into the shrouds and clinging to the mast to avoid being swept into the sea. Over and over a group of rescuers fired the Lyle gun, but always the end of the rope fell short of the floundering vessel.

Night pulled a curtain over the struggle. The storm continued to rage and those on shore built driftwood fires and prayed. In morning's light only six men remained clinging to the shrouds. Exhaustion and the numbing cold continued to take its grim toll. There were four men. Three. Two. One. And finally none.

It was thought all hands had perished but a body, held afloat by a life jacket, washed ashore on the beach instead of being dashed into the rocks. The heart of first assistant engineer Harry Kentzal still beat. He was the lone survivor of the wreck of the *SS Czarina*.

BEESWAX TREASURE

A mysterious landmark on the Pacific is that of Neahkahnie Mountain. It juts from the Oregon coast like a great stone fist, 1,795 feet above the waves that endlessly beat against its exposed flank. Many believe this imposing mountain is the guardian of a priceless treasure.

There are many legends of Neahkahnie. One intriguing tale was related by Indians -- that three strange ships threw smoke and thunder at each other. Two ships drowned and the third limped toward shore, beached itself on the sand and lay there, sails flapping like a mortally wounded gull.

Just as interesting as the Indian legend is the physical evidence which substantiates the theory of a shipwreck. One of the early white men into the area was Alexander Henry of the North West Fur Company. He camped near the mountain in December 1813 and wrote, "The old Clatsop chief arrived with some excellent salmon. There came with him a man about thirty years of age, who had red hair and is the supposed offspring of a survivor of a shipwreck many years ago. Great quantities of beeswax are dug out of the sand near here and the Indians bring it to trade with us."

When the settlers arrived they were told of the Indian legend. They wandered the beach finding chunks of beeswax. In 1892, Dr. C.E. Linton, operator of the drug store in Waldport, collected over two tons of beeswax that had washed ashore after a storm. One piece was shaped like a book on which hieroglyphics were imprinted.

In recent times a chunk of wax marked "1679" in Arabic numerals was found, a date when there was considerable trade between the Orient and South America. It was also a time when pirate ships roamed the seas.

Each Pacific storm brings with it the fresh possibility that more beeswax or perhaps some item from a treasure chest will wash ashore and be found by a beachcomber, adding still more evidence to the belief that long ago a mystery ship wrecked at the foot of Neahkahnie Mountain.

RUM RUNNERS

The Canadian rum runner, *Sea Island*, swung wide to avoid the Coast Guard patrol. With light from a pair of lanterns she made her way toward a secluded harbor a mile north of Depot Bay. At the rock-rimmed entrance she ran aground and tore a hole the length of her engine room.

The gang waited until low tide and unloaded 51 drums of pure alcohol, plus 4 barrels of rum and 275 cases of whiskey. They stashed some of the spirits in a nearby cave and buried more beneath the sand. The gang headed to Portland.

Coastal residents uncovered the cache. A party was in full swing when the state police arrived. They made no arrests but demanded the party-goers carry the booze up the trail where it was loaded on trucks bound for a storeroom in the Toledo city jail.

Shortly after midnight on March 20, two trucks, a Buick sedan, and a Buick coupe drove into Toledo. Two men with machine guns crawled from the coupe. They stood guard while seven others hustled a portable cutting torch into position and cut down the steel jail doors. They loaded the confiscated liquor onto the trucks and tried to escape.

But bad luck still dogged them. One of the trucks stalled. The coupe returned just as two plain-clothed officers arrived. The officers leveled their guns at the coupe and the rum runners gave up without a struggle. They were arrested, stood trial and were sentenced to terms in the state penitentiary. But they did not serve even a single day of their sentence because the National Prohibition Act was repealed on December 5, 1933.

VALUABLE CARGO

In 1848, during a heavy winter storm, the schooner *Woodpecker* went aground on Clatsop Spit. In her hold was a load of flour, flour worth $12 a barrel.

B.C. Kindred had a donation land claim on a bench overlooking the spit. He saw the *Woodpecker* wreck and her crew abandon ship. Once the storm had passed he took his two oldest sons and rowed through the crashing surf to the *Woodpecker*.

They worked on an ebb tide and were successful in breaking through the hatch and removing seven barrels of flour. By that time the tide had changed and waves were breaking over the deck. It was too dangerous to attempt to free any more of the valuable cargo.

During the salvage attempt Mrs. Kindred had impatiently paced back and forth along the beach, praying her men would return safely, that they would be successful in salvaging some of the cargo. She walked, worried, thought about what might be in the ship's hold. There were so many things they needed. Mrs. Kindred squinted -- it appeared a flock of very large geese had landed and were bobbing up and down in the surf between the ship and the beach.

The action of the waves had accomplished what her husband and sons had been unable to do, free the cargo. Flour barrels washed ashore and Mrs. Kindred was kept busy rolling them above the high water mark.

The men rowed to shore, towing their seven barrels of flour. They were greeted by Mrs. Kindred and her 360 barrels.

THE PET WAPITI

Lucy Gould was thrilled when her brothers returned from a trip into the coast mountains with a baby bull elk. She recalled, "I never will forget how little the creature was, so spindly, so sleek, so pretty.

"We fed it cows milk from a bottle until it was strong enough to suck one of our cows, one that would accept him. The orphan calf adjusted to his new mother but as he grew taller he found standing for his dinner inconvenient; it was then necessary for him to take a kneeling position. He soon outgrew that position, too, and so, not to be outdone by a small thing like size, he would lie down to snack."

The cow and the elk, when separated, would communicate; the cow mooing and the elk answering in his peculiar whistling voice. The children called their pet Wapiti, which in the Indian language meant elk. When Wapiti would lie down to rest the children crawled all over him and even stayed on his back as he stood and rode him around. The elk was gentle and seemed to genuinely love the children as much as they loved him.

In time the elk grew horns and then, once in a while, he would chase one of the children when they went to the pasture to bring in the cows. The day finally came when George Gould thought the three-year-old elk too dangerous to keep on the farm.

"The day Wapiti left was sad for us children," remembered Lucy. "Our last moments with him were spent sobbing. We cut a bit of hair off him for a keepsake and then Father led him away. He took Wapiti to the Umpqua Valley and traded him for a horse."

24

HEIFER DUST

The first public school in Coos County began in 1857. For a number of years the school "year" was a three-month session during the summer and, consequently, it was difficult to hold the children's interest.

One time a group of boys learned their teacher was deathly afraid of chipmunks. They tied a live, baby chipmunk to the clapper of the hand bell and replaced it carefully on the teacher's desk. When she went to ring the bell, signaling the end of recess, the chipmunk popped out. She threw the bell and shrieked at the top of her lungs.

Adjoining the school yard was the Bob Herron farm. He raised pigs and one day one of his weaner pigs was smuggled into school and turned loose. The classroom erupted in giggles and a few boys started making grunting sounds. It was a long moment before the teacher grasped that there was a live pig on the loose. She instructed the girls to step outside and had the boys attempt to catch the animal. They grabbed at it as it darted between desks. It was great fun. The boys "just missed" until the middle of the afternoon and the pig was so exhausted it could no longer run.

One of the most serious practical jokes pulled at Coos County Public School #1 was the time cow dung was placed on the seat of the teacher's chair. Fortunately she noticed it before she sat down. She turned slowly to face the class. She fought to control her rising anger. Her face flushed deep red and she spoke in a high-pitched voice. "Who," she demanded to know, "put this...this 'heifer dust' on my chair?"

WORLD'S LARGEST FLAGPOLE

The largest flagpole in the world, a gift from the fine citizens of Astoria, was destined for unveiling in San Francisco.

The fir tree that had been selected as the flagpole was floated south. As it was towed into San Francisco Bay a storm struck and tore it loose. Several days later it was found drifting in a rip tide near Alcatraz Island. The log was lifted from the water and a six-man crew took ten days shaping it into a pole that was 222 feet in length and weighed an estimated 35 tons.

Citizens of Astoria had requested their gift stand free, without cables or guy wires and the raising ceremony aroused a great deal of excitement in the city. A large crowd gathered as ten feet of the butt were set in a 200-ton block of reinforced concrete. Three derricks were positioned to raise the pole. Inch by inch the top came up, until it pointed straight at the sky.

Only a very special flag could be worthy of such a tremendous pole. The women of Astoria had hand-sewn a flag measuring 46 feet in length. The flag was run up the pole and fluttered over the opening ceremony of the 1914 Panama-Pacific International Exposition.

STAYING ALIVE

Four men were crossing from the Rogue River valley to the coast when they became lost. They wandered for more than a week, existing on roots and berries, before stumbling across an Indian with a canoe on the Coquille River.

They bartered for the canoe and paddled it down river to an Indian village. There they became embroiled in a disagreement. Two of them thought they should not risk entering a camp when they did not know if the Indians were friendly. The others said they should make a show of force, fight for food if necessary.

As the discussion went on the canoe drifted into slack water. The Indians did the deciding. They attacked. Two of the white men stayed with the canoe and escaped but the other two leaped into the river. These men, Williams and Hedden, had their troubles. Williams was struck with an arrow and Hedden had to help him to shore where he broke off the shaft and helped his friend to the small settlement of Scottsburg.

Hedden never left Scottsburg. Williams had the arrow surgically removed from his side and went on to become county clerk of Douglas County.

CAST UPON THE WATER

Kenyon Crandall was a seafaring man who, while at home port in Boston, decided to abandon the sea and seek his fortune out west. He came overland in a wagon train, taking the southern route to California. From there he secured passage on the sailing ship *Charles G. Delvin* to Portland.

He arrived the day before Christmas 1852 and disembarked; his first step onto Oregon soil was at the foot of Taylor Street. In a driving snowstorm he walked to Hillsboro. From this tenuous beginning Crandall came to love his adopted state. He forgot the sea and the high masted schooners and turned his attention to farming. For sixty years Kenyon Crandall called Oregon home. Then he died.

The 82-year-old pioneer left specific instructions. According to his wishes his body was cremated and half the ashes were sent to Honolulu, Hawaii where they were scattered on the ocean. The remaining ashes were taken to the foot of Taylor Street and dumped into the Willamette River. Until the ashes find each other in the vast expanse of the Pacific, the spirit of Kenyon Crandall will remain in his adopted state of Oregon.

HIS HONOR'S WHISKERS

Dr. H.L. Henderson had a glorious, bushy beard of perfectly trained black hair. It measured 24 inches wide and 36 inches long and was frosted with just a touch of white like the first dusting of snow at the start of winter.

The doctor claimed he had the finest beard on the Pacific coast and when he was elected mayor of Astoria he proclaimed he had the finest beard of any mayor in the country. As mayor he was a popular figure and during the 1912 Astoria Centennial celebration, the centennial committee made a proposal that brought the city international publicity; they offered free transportation to anyone in the world who had a better set of whiskers than their mayor. There were no serious challengers.

During the celebration the mayor was called on time after time to stand with visiting dignitaries and tourists. Usually it was arranged so he would be standing in the middle of the group where his whiskers would show to their best advantage. Oftentimes the view of those on either side of him would be blocked.

The mayor was a magnificent figure at the official ceremony marking the 100th year of Astoria's existence. His beard flowed over his chest and reached to his knees. But during the lengthy speeches a light drizzle began and his Honor carefully tucked his beard inside his coat. Then he looked very ordinary.

BARE KNUCKLES

Tommy Ward lived in Astoria and was considered one of the toughest men on the coast. On November 2, 1885, he proved just how tough he was in a grueling boxing match.

In those days prize fighting was illegal but news of the scheduled bout spread. On the afternoon of the big fight one thousand fans gathered on the bank of the Lewis River across the Columbia from St. Helens. London rules were in effect: the fight would be bare-knuckled, a round ended when a man was knocked to the ground, and the bout was over when only one man could answer the bell.

Ward met his opponent, a man named Sullivan, in the center of the ring. They shook hands like gentlemen and then got down to the serious business of fighting. They circled like roosters and then Ward unexpectedly rushed in, arms flailing. A bare fist landed on Sullivan's cheek and an elbow crashed into his ribs. He went down. Round one was over.

The bell rang and both men came out swinging. It was a bitter toe-to-toe struggle with Sullivan getting the worst of it.

Finally Sullivan could no longer protect himself. Ward ripped him with two savage blows and Sullivan started down for the last time. On the way he managed to drag his fingers across Ward's face, gouging his eyes and opening a cut on his neck. The spectacle had gone on for a brutal 77 rounds.

31

GOLD OF WHISKEY RUN

The spring of 1852 a band of Indians discovered gold on the Oregon coast. Two white men bought the claim that was yielding up to an ounce of fine gold with every pan. They set up a sluice box and in a very short time took out one hundred thousand dollars worth of gold.

Word of the big strike reached the outside and a gold rush resulted with men flooding in from the Willamette Valley as well as from San Francisco. The beach north of the Coquille River was staked and a thousand miners took up residence in tents. Saloons sprung up overnight. There were wild times for those who found pay dirt.

The best spot proved to be where a small creek flattened out before running into the ocean. The men having claims in this location became fabulously wealthy and their stretch of beach became known as Whiskey Run. One story had it that two Whiskey Run miners filled a five gallon can with gold and, to keep it safe, they packed it up to the headlands and buried it beneath a distinctive tree. Then a fire swept through the area and the cache of gold could never again be located.

Within a year of the gold discovery on the ocean beach the placer deposit had been picked clean. The community was abandoned. The relentless waves of the Pacific slowly began to erase the traces of the miners. Today nothing remains of Whiskey Run.

COUGAR

Sunlight filtered through tall fir trees. Birds sang cheerfully. A small girl and her older brother hurried down the path toward school. The boy, carrying a lunch basket, paused to scold the family dog and send it home.

In the past cougars had screamed from the brushy draw ahead. The girl was afraid and requested of her brother, "Take my hand, please."

"Naw," he told her. "What if someone seen me? 'Sides, you got to grow up an' quit bein' so scared."

"Please." She was close to tears and tried to take his hand, but he pulled away and started walking.

As they descended into the draw the brush crowded in close to the trail. The music of the birds was hushed and the air was dank and stale. The hair on the nape of the brother's neck suddenly stood on end. He whirled around just in time to see a cougar leap from a tree onto his little sister. She screamed. The brother was there beating the cougar with his lunch basket. The cougar turned on the boy, slapped at him and opened several deep gashes on his face.

In the middle of this battle the family dog appeared, snarling, snapping, biting at the cougar. He drove the wild animal away.

The children survived the attack. The cougar was hunted down by a group of local men and was found to be a male so old its teeth were worn down to the gums.

TILLAMOOK ROCK

The Tillamook lighthouse sits on a pile of rock only 100 feet long and 80 feet wide. And on this tiny, barren island lived a keeper and four assistants. Women were not allowed.

Once a month a lighthouse tender would land bringing supplies, letters and news from the mainland. Between visits the men stationed at the lighthouse read, played music, target practiced and scrubbed and cleaned the lighthouse windows and walls.

Not every man was suited to the lonely existence on the rock. In 1890 a man named Zauer went crazy after having spent three years on the rock. He died in a Salem insane asylum. Another time one of the men stationed at the lighthouse became obsessed with jealousy and was convinced that his wife on the mainland was being unfaithful to him. He stole the emergency boat, rowed the one and one-half miles through the strong and treacherous current to shore. The story had a happy ending. He visited his wife, discovered she was still true, and then he returned to the rock.

The light at the Tillamook lighthouse was turned off September 1, 1957. The rock was given back to the sea gulls and the crashing waves. Today the tower remains as a symbol to the men who risked their lives, and sanity, to keep the light burning.

FOOL CROSSING

The Parker family immigrated to the Oregon coast in the fall of 1889. They were from the landlocked state of South Dakota and Parker, wanting his children to be near the ocean, took a homestead on the south side of Yaquina Bay.

The family stayed in Newport. Parker camped on the homestead and hurried to build a cabin so they could be settled before winter. By the first of November he had completed the bare essentials and made arrangements to have a man in Newport ferry the family to their new home.

It was a sunny day when they departed Newport and the ocean was beginning to calm from a storm that had passed during the night. As Parker got ready to shove the rowboat away an old sailor came to the dock and warned them, "Don't go. The ocean looks flat but it's not." He also pointed out that a rowboat carrying three adults and seven children, showing very little freeboard, was dangerous. Despite the concern of the sailor Parker shoved away and the boatman began rowing.

"Fools," the sailor called after them. He hiked up on a bluff overlooking the ocean and watched the terrible tragedy unfold. He saw the tiny rowboat dip into a wave, be lifted and dropped. Mrs. Parker and her seven children were swallowed by the cold sea. The men, neither of whom could swim, struggled to stay on the surface.

Rescuers found only one survivor, Parker, clinging to the overturned rowboat. The following morning the tide washed the body of Mrs. Parker ashore. Her youngest child was still clutched in her arms.

EASY SCALP

The Puyallup and Nisqually Indian tribes were not on friendly terms. One day a Nisqually brave came bursting into the cabin of Puget Sound pioneer Peter Smith, pleading, "Hide me!" The words were barely out of his mouth when a number of Puyallups appeared in the doorway and demanded the brave, saying they were going to scalp him.

"Hold it a minute," Smith stated coolly. "Why be in such a rush? I have a proposition."

Smith had been a champion runner as a boy in his homeland of Scotland. He proposed to take responsibility for the Nisqually, to train him to run; and at the end of two weeks there would be a footrace to determine if the Puyallups were worthy to lift the scalp of the Nisqually.

The agreement was struck and as soon as the Puyallups had departed Smith began training the brave. He taught the young man how to breathe properly, how to swing his arms to lengthen his stride and how to run on the balls of his feet. He worked on conditioning, sending the Indian to the top of the largest rise around, Melville Springs Hill. Time after time he climbed the hill.

On the day of the footrace a large congregation of Puyallups set camp near Smith's cabin. The runners took their positions. The Nisqually was given a head start of one hundred yards, according to the agreement Smith had worked out, before the Puyallups were allowed to give chase. Straight up the steep incline of Melville Springs Hill ran the Nisqually, arms and legs pumping like pistons, while his pursuers lagged behind. At the top he paused, waved a good-bye to his trainer and broke over the far side.

TURKEY WOMAN

Miss Arda Edwards began a career teaching school but gave that up to become the "Turkey Woman".

"I made $540 a year teaching and this year will clear $1,100 with my turkeys," said Miss Edwards. "Not a single woman teacher in this county makes that and only eight men teachers make more."

Her turkey flock began with twenty hens and two toms purchased in the fall of 1913. The next year she sold 250 turkeys and kept 40 hens.

"My formula for success is simple," said Miss Edwards. "Keep the finest birds for breeding, be sure they stay healthy and give them plenty of room."

Miss Edwards owned a 700-acre farm in the coast range and allowed her flock to roam. She spent most days guarding her precious turkeys like a good dog guards sheep.

"My day starts before the sun is up," she commented. "I have my breakfast and hike up the hill about a mile from my house. Usually I locate my turkeys on that hill.

"During the day the turkeys go where the grasshoppers tend to congregate. Come night I leave them in the trees while I go home to rest a bit.

"I make friends with my birds. I spend time picking out names. There is Tetrazzini -- she sings, Gentle Lady, Whispering Hen, The Goat, Silver Maple...."

The natural enemy of turkeys on open range includes everything that can walk, crawl or slither. Miss Edwards protected her flock from skunks, weasels, hogs, dogs, and rattlesnakes.

"Of the months of the year I much prefer March because the babies are hatching. September is by far the worst month. I have to help with the killing. I don't care for killing, but then comes the money and I do care for that."

GRANDPA'S STORY

Grandpa was born in New Brunswick and before he turned 25 he had fought with McClellan in the Civil War and had driven an ox team across the continent.

The Pacific Ocean stopped him and he settled at the forward tip of a large bay. The surrounding mountains were covered with virgin forests of Douglas fir and Grandpa became a logger. For years he operated his own outfit and when he finally retired there was nothing he enjoyed more that sitting around, grandchildren scattered at his feet, telling stories of the early days.

"Used to cross the bay in Indian canoes," he was fond of telling. "That was the only way to get to the other side except to hike fifty miles and the trails them days was mighty poor.

"Worse crossin' I ever remember come about ... now I ain't sure exact dates, but I remember well enough what happened. It was winter, bad storm comin' our way. It was the worse time in the world for Grandma to pick to get sick. Boy, was she sick! I knew I had to get her 'cross the bay to the settlement, have the doctor treat 'er. So I grabbed my ax, a good logger is never without his ax, and I commenced walkin'.

"When I got to the Indian village there was better 'n a dozen ocean-goin' canoes pulled on shore. The Indians was havin' some kind of feast. I asked nice and polite like if they'd be so kind as to ferry me and my missus 'cross. They acted like they couldn't understand. I spoke Chinook, even offered to pay. No dice. They had their bellies full of fish and the water was already rough. 'Sides, what was one white man going to do?

"I thought for a minute, marched straight to a canoe, started choppin' with my ax. I was on the second canoe and goin' strong when they stopped me and agreed to ferry us 'cross. Seems we spoke the same language after all."

TAKING ON A WHALE

The ship *Umatilla* was on a southern course bound for the Columbia. Sighting an approaching ship Captain Worth signaled, asking if they had any recent newspapers aboard. The ship ranged alongside and one of the crew tossed a copy of the *Oregonian* onto the deck of the *Umatilla*.

Captain Worth glanced through the shipping intelligence and was perusing the local columns when he was roused by a violent jarring of the ship. It was followed by a quick thunderclap and one of the crewman hollered, "Captain, we hit a whale. There, he breaks water!"

Off to starboard the ocean was crimson. The whale wallowed on the surface, then with a tremendous slap of his tail he dove. The monster was not seen again until three days later when its carcass washed up on shore at the entrance to Shoalwater Bay. It attracted a great deal of attention and many tourists came to have their pictures taken with the whale. After a few days in the hot sun the whale began to smell. Still the public flocked to see the creature.

One fellow, to impress several girls, climbed onto the back of the whale and stood there delivering a lengthy oratory, gesturing wildly with his arms. Suddenly his footing gave way and he dropped straight into the mountain of decaying blubber.

When he finally was able to extricate himself, soaked with the pungent odor of the whale, he told his friends that next time he would prefer to make an entrance as Jonah had and take his chances on being digested.

HIRED MAN

Bronte Coffelt Smith grew up along the Oregon coast and recalled that back in the late 1800s his father would occasionally hire a man to help during harvest.

"One year a man came to our house and wanted work," said Smith. "It was during potato diggin' and apple pickin' and we were short-handed. I remember Father saying he didn't much care for the fellow's appearance but like I said, we were short-handed.

"Father was a little afraid to have him stay in the house with us and so he informed him that he would have to bunk in the barn. He slept in the hayloft and ate his meals with us. Sometimes at dinner he would mumble things to himself, carry on a general discourse, and then laugh and laugh. Father would ask him, 'What are you laughing about, Fred?' And Fred would shrug, answer, 'I don't know,' and go right on laughing.

"After several weeks of this strange behavior my folks realized Fred was crazy, but he was such a good worker they hated to let him go. Finally the issue resolved itself. This one evening a big thunderstorm came in and Fred acted crazier than ever. He even told Father, 'I better leave here tonight or someone might get hurt. I don't want to hurt anyone.'

"Father persuaded Fred to go to bed in the hayloft. Once he got up there Father took away the ladder and called the sheriff.

"Turned out Fred fit the description of a dangerous man who had escaped the asylum over in Salem. The sheriff took one look and said Fred was the man. That was it -- we all had to pitch in and work harder for losing the hired man."

41

STRANGE MUSIC

The James family were among the first settlers on the north Pacific coast. They claimed homestead ground and built a log cabin facing the broad, sparkling ocean.

One morning fourteen-year-old Mary happened to glance westward and caught the quick flash of sunlight on paddles. As she watched, two Indian canoes came into view making for the landing on the beach below the cabin.

"Mother!" cried Mary. "Indians are coming!"

In short order thirty braves were crowded into the small cabin. They walked around picking up things: a spyglass, salt and pepper shakers, a small porcelain statue. They grunted and showed off each new discovery. Always the items were returned to their proper places. In time one of the Indians, using a mixture of Chinook jargon and English, wanted to know where the man of the house was.

"The men will return soon, any minute," lied Mrs. James. Her husband and sons were away cutting hay in a meadow and would not return until late afternoon.

An idea came to her. "Mary, please play something pretty on the melodeon for our guests. Play now."

Mary took a seat on the stool, faced the melodeon. She was too nervous to play well, but play she did. The Indians were awestruck by the music and got down on their hands and knees trying to find the source of the strange sound.

In fact, the Indians were so charmed by Mary and her music they presented a great quantity of hiaqua shells (Indian money), and laid them on the table with woven grass mats, baskets and fish. They made it evident they wished to purchase the wonderful melodeon as well as the girl who made it work.

"Oh gracious! Oh, my goodness, no!" came Mrs. James's quick reply. To appease them she cut squares from a bolt of bright red cloth she had been saving for a dress, gave each Indian a present and sent them on their way.

GRANDPA

His given name was James R. DeVaul but everyone called him Grandpa.

Grandpa was born in Kentucky in 1814 but was reared on the Missouri frontier. He married Sarah Howell in 1837 and went into the general merchandising business. Half a century later, after having fathered 12 children, Grandpa decided to move the family to the West Coast, saying he wanted his children and grandchildren to live the "Oregon Dream".

The DeVaul family settled on the southern Oregon coast and Grandpa built a large house. He hunted and fished to put meat on the table and tended a big garden. Added to that subsistence was a small pension he received for having been a veteran of the Black Hawk War.

The coastal climate stimulated Grandpa. Except for his snow-white hair and beard he was the perfect picture of youthful exuberance. His normal day started well before sunrise with milking and various chores. Later he would help a neighbor or go off into the woods to hunt or up the river to fish.

Grandpa celebrated his 80th birthday by shooting a deer and packing it home on his shoulders. At 90 he hiked upriver and returned with a fine mess of fish; 92 and his eyesight was still so good he continued to read without glasses.

One Sunday afternoon, in November 1906, while visiting the nearby home of one of his daughters, Grandpa closed his eyes. Life flew away.

BEAR AND THE BOY

Eras Rosecrans lived with his parents in the foothills of the Coast range. One fall afternoon the boy was hunting near home, walking slowly, quietly, on the lookout for fresh sign.

He had rounded a brushy thicket when he spotted a large black bear not more than thirty paces away sitting on its haunches eating berries. Eras very slowly raised his rifle and pointed it at the bear. As his trigger finger curled, fear coursed through his veins. What if he only wounded the bear? Kerbamm! The boy did not stick around to see what happened next. He dropped the gun and ran. Ran like the wind. And behind him he could hear the bear crashing through the brush, closer, closer, could hear its heavy breathing. A branchy tree was just ahead and Eras grabbed a low limb, swung up and climbed.

Eras stayed in the tree, and not having seen any sign of the bear after an hour he got up the nerve to come down. His feet hit the ground running. Again he could hear the bear chasing him even over the sound of his own pounding heart, could feel the hot breath of the bear on the nape of his neck. He dared not look back, kept running.

At last he made it home, too out of breath to tell his father and brother what had happened. When he was finally able to speak he told the story, about shooting the bear and only wounding it, how the enraged beast had chased him all the way to the clearing where their cabin sat. Eras, his father and brother returned to the spot where Eras had shot the bear and there it was, dead.

DISCOVERY

Elijah Davidson and his faithful dog Bruno were on a hunting expedition in the Siskiyou Mountains. They were working a long, steep ridge when Bruno flushed a deer. Elijah fired. The deer went down.

While Elijah was gutting his deer Bruno continued to hunt. He was soon barking scent; from his excited tone it sounded as though he were hot on the trail of a bear. Elijah cleaned his knife by wiping it on the deer's hide and then joined in the chase. He crawled over rocks and windfalls following a string of fading barks. When he could no longer hear Bruno, he continued in the general direction.

He worked his way to an outcropping of mossy, gray rocks, to where a small stream gushed from a narrow opening. He bent for a drink from the cold water and again he heard Bruno, but this time the sound seemed to be coming from inside the mountain. Elijah stepped near the opening and could clearly hear a struggle, Bruno growling, snarling, snapping teeth, and the bear roaring in rage. Elijah slipped inside and followed the creek into absolute blackness.

At length he withdrew a block of sulfur matches, broke off a small square and lit it. Flickering yellow light revealed a large cave leading still deeper into the mountain. Shadows played across strange shapes. And then it was dark again.

Elijah continued until his supply of sulfur was nearly exhausted. With dark pressing in he started back, walking, sometimes crawling on hands and knees in the small stream, allowing it to lead him to the outside world.

When at last he reached the entrance the late afternoon was coloring a rainbow in the mist. He scrambled toward the light, basked in it, allowed it to warm him. He waited there at the entrance for Bruno to come out. In time he did.

The underground cavern became known as Elijah Caves, later as Marble Halls and then Josephine Caves. In 1909 President Taft signed legislation making the caves a national monument and officially naming them the Oregon Caves.

WRECK OF THE *WARREN*

The *SS General Warren* was a 309-ton side-wheel steamer built in Portland, Maine. She was in service for eight years along the New England coast until beckoned around Cape Horn by the gold strike at Sutter's Mill in California.

The *Warren* unloaded would-be miners in San Francisco and then was pressed into duty carrying passengers and cargo along the Pacific coast. One of her frequent ports of call was the small settlement of Portland, Oregon. She was there in January 1852 taking on a load of grain.

On the day she departed a few passengers embarked, the lines were cast away and the *Warren* slipped into the current. As she entered the Columbia and turned toward the sea a brisk wind blew and the sky became dark and threatening. Nearing the mouth of the Columbia the western sky appeared as a solid sheet of blue-black clouds. The *Warren* was swept toward the bar and she pitched and rolled on the swells, the paddle wheel at times completely out of the water and at other times nearly submerged. She crossed into the open sea, setting a southwesterly course.

The storm overran the *Warren,* the sky dropped a torrent of rain; the wind blew a gale. The ship rose high on sweeping waves and slid out of sight in deep troughs. White spume danced. Sea spray was driven by the violent wind. For the crew and passengers it was a terror-filled night.

The light of a new day revealed the *Warren* in trouble and in danger of sinking. The captain gave the order to swing the wheel hard up and set a course due east. The steamer struck the Clatsop Spit; the captain ordered a single lifeboat and ten of his best men to cast away and seek help.

The lifeboat managed to reach Astoria, but before a rescue party could be dispatched the sea had claimed the *Warren*. In all, 42 persons lost their lives. Among the bodies that washed ashore was a young married couple, their hands locked together in death as they had been in life.

TO VOTE

Lou Southworth was born a slave in Kentucky. He came to Oregon in 1851, worked in several Jacksonville mines and eventually moved into a cabin near the mouth of the Alsea River. On Election Day 1864, he announced, "Mr. Lincoln is on trial in this election. I am going to vote."

A big storm hit the coast that day. In order to vote, Lou would have to cross Alsea Bay to reach the town of Waldport. Friends told him, "You'll never make it," but Lou said he owed it to President Lincoln at least to try.

Lou went to work securing empty oil barrels to his rowboat in the hope they would protect him from capsizing. As he shoved off a small crowd gathered; none gave him a ghost of a chance of making it.

The small boat was tossed on the waves and all the while Lou pulled with the oars. For a short time the boat was lost from sight and then someone shouted, "There he is!" It was clear to see Lou had passed the area of most danger and had entered calmer water.

Lou succeeded in reaching Waldport where he voted straight Republican. He was the only man from the other side of the bay to vote in the election.

PORT ORFORD METEORITE

One of the great mysteries of the Pacific coast had its origins in the year Oregon became a state - 1859. Noted federal geologist, Dr. John Evans, was collecting mineral specimens from the West and one of his samples, assayed by an eastern laboratory, was determined to have come from a meteorite.

Dr. Evans was notified and immediately consulted his notes. The sample had been taken from a spot roughly 40 miles east of the settlement of Port Orford, on the west slope of Bald Mountain. Dr. Evans calculated from his field measurements that the source rock would weigh approximately 22,000 pounds, making it the largest meteorite found, up to that time, in the United States.

Dr. Evans appeared before Congress to ask that funds be appropriated to organize an expedition to locate and transport the meteorite from Oregon to Washington, D.C. But before the funds were committed the Civil War erupted and then Dr. Evans died.

In the ensuing years geologists, miners and weekend prospectors have attempted to retrace Dr. Evans's footsteps. They have crisscrossed the west slope of Bald Mountain but no one has located the resting spot of the Port Orford meteorite. To this day it remains hidden in the folds of the Coast range.

STORM TO END ALL STORMS

May 4, 1880 dawned with a gentle breeze fanning the ocean and making ideal conditions for commercial fishing. Hundreds of fishing boats were trolling for salmon at the entrance to the Columbia River.

Without forewarning a wild wind began, turning the peaceful swells into a boiling cauldron. The wind hit one hundred miles an hour and boats swamped, capsized and sank.

Most major storms move onto the coast from the south or west but this wind came out of the northwest. It was localized at the mouth of the Columbia and raged for thirty terrifying minutes, then stopped as suddenly as it began. The air became quiet, the sea flat. Nowhere was there a boat to be seen.

It was estimated 240 boats went down in the storm and loss of life was set at 325. Those were only statistics. For weeks after the disaster families and friends of the deceased walked the beaches, searching through the debris that washed up on shore -- nets, splinters of wood, trolling poles and other fishing gear -- for some sign of their loved ones. And the ocean, it showed not the slightest remorse.

50

THE *FEARLESS*

She was built in Shanghai of teakwood, christened the *Star Of China* and used in the opium trade. She sailed the Pacific until 1852 when she was seized by police in San Francisco and sold at public auction. The new owner installed a steam engine, rechristened her *Fearless* and established her home port as North Bend, Oregon.

At three in the afternoon on October 13, 1873, the *Fearless* departed Camman's Wharf at North Bend under the guidance of Captain James Hill and a crew of four. The weather was clear, the ocean calm; but as *Fearless* crossed the bar a groundswell rose and rocked the vessel. Captain Hill advanced the throttle. Suddenly the safety valve blew from the steam boiler.

The *Fearless* was adrift without power and Captain Hill was quick to order, "Drop anchor."

"We're dragging," hollered the engineer.

An onshore breeze began blowing and Captain Hill, hoping to escape danger, ordered the sails put up. The crew frantically worked but just as they began tacking, the wind died.

The *Fearless* drifted and at nightfall the captain and crew knew their only hope for survival was to stay with the ship. In the distance the lights from the settlement of Charleston twinkled brightly. The noise of the waves crashing on shore grew in intensity. Finally the ship went aground, groaned and lay on her side. Waves washed over her. Captain Hill led the way, swimming and wading to shore, pulling a heaving line, and the crew followed. They abandoned the *Fearless*.

TAKING THE ROGUE

The year was 1855 and the Shasta tribe was trying to live in peace on the Table Rock Reservation of southern Oregon. William Guin, a white man, was even building a frame house for the chief, Chief John.

But October 8 dawned blood red with a group of miners poised to attack two reservation camps. They were out to revenge an act of cattle rustling alleged to have been committed by Indians.

On a prearranged signal the white men began firing into the first sleeping village and managed to kill eight men and fifteen women and children in the volley. The survivors were persuaded to surrender. When they laid down their weapons they were shot.

In a simultaneous attack on the second village a woman was killed and another woman and two boys were critically wounded. During this quick battle one of the organizers of the ambush, James Lupton, stumbled across an Indian he thought was dead. But the brave, using his feet to hold the bow, pulled back on the string and released an obsidian-tipped arrow into Lupton's rib cage. He died instantly.

Chief John gathered the remainder of his people and organized Indians along the Rogue River. He led an attack against the white settlements in the area and with his own hands killed William Guin, saying as he murdered him, "Chief John want no house. I fight until I die."

Eighteen months later Chief John, with only 25 able-bodied warriors remaining, was forced to surrender. From that day on, the Rogue country belonged to the white man.

THE PARDON

Tillamook's first jail was nothing more than a shack of fir logs covered with crude wooden shakes. One of the first guests was a hog stealer. Anyway, some folks claimed he was a hog stealer. He maintained he was not.

One night the man escaped and the next day he casually strolled into the offices of *The Oregon Statesman* in Salem. He told the editor, "I've been done a great injustice. I was arrested and convicted in Tillamook for hog stealing. But I'm not guilty. Bears ate those hogs. I just can't prove it.

"Now," he reasoned, "I'm your only subscriber in Tillamook and I demand you obtain a pardon for me from the governor, or ... or ... I'll cancel my subscription."

A paying subscriber was highly valued. A meeting with Governor Gibbs was requested and the governor listened to the convicted man tell his side of the story.

"But if you were convicted in Tillamook, sentenced to jail, how in the world did you get here, in my office?" the governor wanted to know.

"Easy," replied the man. "I just crawled up the inside logs, pushed the shakes aside and jumped off the roof. And now, Governor, my pardon, please."

The governor shook his head, explained there was nothing he could do until he saw a transcript of the trial. The fugitive explained, "No one did any writing at my trial. The justice of the peace simply listened to the hog owners and I ended up in jail. I never even got to mention about the bears."

The governor thought for a minute and suggested a solution.

"Perhaps I could write a letter on your behalf suggesting you may have been imprisoned without due process of the law."

"That would be every bit as good as a pardon," smiled the man in triumph. "No one in Tillamook is going to have any idea what 'due process of the law' means. Yep, good as a pardon."

CURE FOR BALDNESS

Grandpa and Grandma Keith were early day settlers on the Pacific coast and grandson Herbert Keith related, "They lived in a little cabin way back in the woods. One day a squaw wandered in and asked Grandma if she could borrow a kettle to heat a mixture she said would grow hair on her papoose's head.

"Grandma invited the squaw in, gave her permission to use an old kettle and observed each step. The squaw poured the contents of a small brown vial and several cups of water into the kettle. She added small pieces of wood to the cookstove to build a hot fire and brought the liquid to a rolling boil as she fiercely stirred circles. The concoction gave forth a rather pungent odor and Grandma asked if the recipe perhaps included pumpkin. The squaw shook her head no and set the kettle aside to cool. When the mixture had reached the proper temperature she dabbed it on the head of her papoose.

"Grandma asked the squaw if she could have a bit of the recipe to try on her husband's bald head. The squaw generously agreed, gave Grandma half of what remained.

"That night, when Grandpa came in, Grandma made him sit in the chair and told him he must not move.

"Over his strong objection she smeared his head with the warm, sticky, smelly stuff and told him to leave it on all night and the next day if he wanted a full head of hair. Well, Grandpa did grump about it but he wanted hair awful bad.

"Next morning the squaw returned and Grandpa happened to meet up with her. He asked her what the ingredients of the recipe happened to be and she answered it included a variety of berry juices as well as the bodies of three frogs which had been allowed to stand in the sun until they were reduced to a liquid.

"These words were barely out of the squaw's mouth before Grandpa was running for the spring. It was a full week before he and Grandma were back on speaking terms."

BABY WHALE EXHIBIT

In 1873 a baby whale was observed in the Columbia River, stranded on a sandbar at Chinook Point. Some local boys vowed to turn the carcass into money. Their only problem was deciding whether to bring paying customers to the whale or to take the whale to paying customers, and how to go about it.

One of the boys had an idea. "Let's float 'im, " he said. "We can dig a channel from the high water mark to the whale. It would only have to be a couple hundred feet."

The boys dug a channel and as the tide came in the tugboat *Sedalia* stood offshore while the boys fastened a line from her and looped it around the whale's tail. The *Sedalia* took up the slack and the 30-foot-long baby whale began moving.

The *Sedalia* towed the mammal up the Columbia and up the Willamette River. As she pulled into the Portland dock the boys were waiting. They had made all the necessary arrangements and the whale was lifted and set in the back of the sturdiest wagon in town. It was taken to a warehouse where the boys went to work carving off the thick blubber; some was sold and the remainder went to neighborhood dogs.

The baby whale was reduced to a skeleton. The skeleton was exhibited to paying customers at the Oregon Museum.

ONE SHOT

Oscar Lundberg was known up and down the Coast range as a hunter, trapper and man of the mountains. His busiest time of year was winter, when the weather was cold and furs in prime.

As Oscar tramped around in the snow he always had his dogs, a pack of hounds, with him and when they cut fresh track they bawled to high heaven. The chase was on.

One day Oscar was easing along a creek bottom checking traps, dogs at heel. The wind changed a bit and the dogs caught scent of a wild animal. They howled, ran up a side hill and bayed at the entrance of a cave.

Oscar kicked his dogs out of the way, bent and peered into the dark hole. The only way to identify what was in there was to go inside. He withdrew his pistol and thrust it in front of him as he inched forward. Something grabbed the barrel of the pistol! Shook it fiercely!

Oscar's natural instinct caused him to pull the trigger. There was a quick roar, a ball of fire and then darkness. He waited a moment and proceeded. Much to his surprise he discovered he had interrupted the sleep of a two-year-old bear. It lay on the floor of the cave, dead, shot in the mouth.

57

SEA MEETS SAGE

The ocean-going vessel, *Charles L. Wheeler, Jr.*, came 200 miles inland on July 11, 1938, making the first time in history that The Dalles could brag about being a seaport.

The *Charles L. Wheeler, Jr.*, 300 feet long, had a difficult time navigating the S turns and the tricky Columbia currents. But the ship made it and tied up to the dock in The Dalles while a crowd of ten thousand gathered. Oregon Governor Martin officially opened the river and during his speech made reference to the wonders of Bonneville Dam and the locks that made it possible for ships to reach eastern Oregon. He referred to the historic run as being from "the sea to the sage".

Captain Robert Gray, in May 1792, discovered the "Great River of the West" and named it after his ship, the *Columbia*. Forty-four years later the first steamship, the *Beaver*, ran the river. The *Charles L. Wheeler, Jr.*, had taken its place in history alongside the *Columbia* and *Beaver*. But according to experienced rivermen the real test for the big ship was not in pushing its way inland. The real test would come when it turned seaward and ran with the current.

The *Charles L. Wheeler, Jr.*, unloaded a cargo of asphalt, sugar, salad oil and automobiles and took on wheat, cattle and fruit. On the way down river the ship successfully ran the most dangerous stretch, the swift, narrow channel at the Bridge of the Gods, and was lowered through the Bonneville locks, the largest in the world. By 7 p.m. the *Charles L. Wheeler, Jr.*, was tying up in Vancouver after having crossed the Cascade mountain range twice.

Rick Steber's Tales of the Wild West Series is available in hardbound books ($12.50) and paperback books ($4.95) featuring illustrations by Don Gray, as well as in cassette tapes ($9.95) narrated by Dallas McKennon. A complete teacher study guide for the Tales of the Wild West Series is also available ($8.95). Current titles in the series include:

- ☐   Vol. 1   *Oregon Trail*
- ☐   Vol. 2   *Pacific Coast*
- ☐   Vol. 3   *Indians*
- ☐   Vol. 4   *Cowboys*
- ☐   Vol. 5   *Women of the West*
- ☐   Vol. 6   *Children's Stories*
- ☐   Vol. 7   *Loggers*
- ☐   Vol. 8   *Mountain Men*
- ☐   Vol. 9   *Miners*
- ☐   Vol. 10   *Grandpa's Stories*
- ☐   Vol. 11   *Pioneers*

If unavailable at retailers in your area write directly to the publisher. A catalog describing other books by Rick Steber is free upon request.

Bonanza Publishing
Box 204
Prineville, Oregon 97754